P9-DFR-196

There's NO Such Thing as a DRAGON

Withdrawn

There's NO Such Thing as a DRAGON

Jack Kent

A Golden Book • New York
Golden Books Publishing Company, Inc., New York, New York 10106

jpl
BATAVIA LIBRARY DISTRICT
BATAVIA, ILLINOIS

Billy Bixbee was rather surprised when he woke up one morning and found a dragon in his room. It was a small dragon, about the size of a kitten.

The dragon wagged its tail happily when Billy patted its head.

Billy went downstairs to tell his mother.

"There's no such thing as a dragon!" said Billy's mother. And she said it like she meant it.

Billy went back to his room and began to dress. The dragon came close to Billy and wagged its tail. But Billy didn't pat it. If there's no such thing as something, it's silly to pat it on the head.

Billy washed his face and hands and went down to breakfast. The dragon went along. It was bigger now, almost the size of a dog.

Billy sat down at the table.

The dragon sat down *on* the table.

This sort of thing was not usually permitted, but there wasn't much Billy's mother could do about it. She had already said there was no such thing as a dragon. And if there's no such thing, you can't very well tell it to get down off the table.

Billy washed his face and hands and went down to breakfast. The dragon went along. It was bigger now, almost the size of a dog.

Billy sat down at the table.

The dragon sat down *on* the table.

This sort of thing was not usually permitted, but there wasn't much Billy's mother could do about it. She had already said there was no such thing as a dragon. And if there's no such thing, you can't very well tell it to get down off the table.

Mother made some pancakes for Billy, but the dragon ate them all.

Mother made some more.
But the dragon ate those, too.

Mother kept making pancakes until she ran out of batter.

Billy got only one of them, but he said that's all he really wanted, anyway.

Billy went upstairs to brush his teeth. Mother started clearing the table. The dragon, who was nearly as big as Mother by this time, made himself comfortable on the hall rug and went to sleep.

By the time Billy came back downstairs, the dragon had grown so much he filled the hall. Billy had to go around by way of the living room to get to where his mother was.

"I didn't know dragons grew so fast!" said Billy.

"There's no such thing as a dragon!" said Mother firmly.

Cleaning the downstairs took Mother all morning, what with the dragon in the way . . .

and having to climb in and out of windows to get from room to room.

By noon the dragon filled the house. Its head hung out the front door, its tail hung out the back door, and there wasn't a room in the house that didn't have some part of the dragon in it.

MAIL

When the dragon awoke from his nap, he was hungry.

A bakery truck went by. The smell of fresh bread was more than the dragon could resist.

The dragon ran down the street after the bakery truck.

The house went along, of course, like the shell on a snail.

The mailman was just coming up the path with some mail for the Bixbees when their house rushed past him and headed down the street.

He chased the Bixbees' house for a few blocks, but he couldn't catch it.

When Mr. Bixbee came home for lunch, the first thing he noticed was that the house was gone.

Luckily, one of the neighbors was able to tell him which way it went.

Mr. Bixbee got into his car and went looking for the house. He studied all the houses as he drove along.

Finally, he saw one that looked familiar. Billy and Mrs. Bixbee were waving from an upstairs window.

Mr. Bixbee climbed over the dragon's head, onto the porch roof, and through the upstairs window.

"How did this happen?" Mr. Bixbee asked.

"It was the dragon," said Billy.

"There's no such thing . . ." Mother started to say.

"There *is* a dragon!" Billy insisted. "A very BIG dragon!" And Billy patted the dragon on the head.

The dragon wagged its tail happily. Then, even faster than it had grown, the dragon started getting smaller.

Soon it was kitten-size again.

"I don't mind dragons *this* size," said Mother. "Why did it have to grow so BIG?"

"I'm not sure," said Billy, "but I think it just wanted to be noticed."

DRAGON

Jack Kent *(1920-1985)*

moved many times when he was growing up, traveling with his family from coast to coast. When he was a teenager, he left high school and with no professional art training, began work as a freelance artist and cartoonist. His love of humor and his desire to spread it far and wide were evident early in his career; his syndicated comic strip, "King Aroo," delighted readers for the fifteen years it was published.

Mr. Kent began writing and illustrating books for children in the 1960s, and his fun-loving nature, infectious humor, and enthusiasm are clearly evident in his work. One of Mr. Kent's objectives—to make book lovers out of young readers by giving them books that are fun—was certainly achieved, for what could be more fun than the great big pet dragon in this story!

Copyright 1975 by Golden Books Publishing Company, Inc.
All rights reserved. Printed in Hong Kong.
No part of this book may be reproduced or copied
in any form without written permission from the publisher.
GOLDEN BOOKS®, A GOLDEN BOOK®,
GOLDEN BOOKS FAMILY STORYTIME™, and G DESIGN®
are trademarks of Golden Books Publishing Company, Inc.
10 9 8 7 6 5 4 3 2 1

Library of Congress Cataloging-in-Publication Data
Kent, Jack, 1920.
There's no such thing as a dragon / Jack Kent.
p. cm.
Summary: Billy Bixbee's mother won't admit that dragons
exist until it is nearly too late.
ISBN 0-307-10214-9 (alk. paper)
[1. Dragons—Fiction.] I. Title.
PZ7.K414 Th 2001 [E]—dc21 00-046253